THE CASE OF THE CRUNCHY PEANUT BUTTER

By J.M. Goodspeed

Illustrated by Gilbert Riswold

Xerox Education Publications

XEROX

Text copyright © 1975 by Jeanne Vestal
Illustrations copyright © 1975 by Xerox Corporation

Publishing, Executive and Editorial Offices:
Xerox Education Publications
Middletown, Connecticut 06457

ISBN 0-88375-209-3

Library of Congress Catalogue Card Number: 74-28780

Weekly Reader Children's Book Club Edition
XEROX® is a trademark of Xerox Corporation.

THE CASE OF
THE CRUNCHY
PEANUT BUTTER

Andy kicked the case.

"What'd you do that for?" her brother, Ted, asked. He was calmly munching some candy. As always, he was so matter of fact.

"Because I'm bored stamping jars and filling shelves and I wish something exciting would happen around here," answered Andy.

"Well, at least you've got a job and a steady income. That's more than I've got."

"Ted, you know Pop won't let you work here in the store until you're at least ten, so just relax. Enjoy yourself. It's not that much fun."

"Sure, but you've got that nice pay envelope every Saturday, and I have to ask for everything I want. Every time I need money for anything the whole family has a big pow-wow. It would be great to do something just once on my own say-so."

Andy leaned against the freezer counter and for a little second felt sorry for Ted. For some reason there was a big difference between being nine and being eleven. But there were a lot of things wrong with being eleven, too.

"Yeah," Andy said, "I remember, the allowance is never enough. Do you need something now? I could give you fifty cents or so."

"No, it's just my general state that's so bad, but it might be worse, I suppose. Have a piece of fudge? It's from the school cafeteria."

"Maybe I will, if Mom can't see." Andy blew a black bang out of her eye as she wondered for the hundredth time why she had cut them. She sure couldn't have bangs in her eyes all the time if she was going to be a butcher like her father.

The Millbury Market was the family store. Her father ran the meat counter and the stock, and her mother worked the checkout counter. It was the only store in town, so they had lots of business.

Ted left and Andy went on with her job. She was almost finished stamping the crate of peanut butter when her father came down the aisle.

"Hi, Andy. How are you doing?" He looked down over her shoulder. "Are you sure you've got that price right, Kitten? Seems to me it went up. Where's the sheet?"

Andy drew out the price sheet, feeling very smart.

"That's the old one, Andy. I'm sure it's fifty-one cents on the small size now."

Andy didn't even like crunchy peanut butter, and twice through the same box of jars was too much. She threw down the stamp and stomped off to the back room. She knew she'd have to re-mark the jars, but a drink of orange and a walk around the back would help.

Her father caught up with her in the cooler. "I'm sorry, Kitten, but you've got to get that case out of the aisle. I know it's no fun, but it's a help here."

That's why Andy remembered she'd marked a whole case of crunchy peanut butter—twice over. Less than a week later she found herself with another whole new case. Andy knew there weren't enough people in Millbury to buy and eat that much in one week.

She went looking for her father and found him in the little office, doing his usual Sunday paper work.

"Pop, what happened to all the peanut butter I put on the shelf just the other day?"

"We must have sold it. Didn't I reorder?" Her father answered without much interest.

"Yes, but that's not what I mean. I put out a whole new case last Wednesday afternoon. Don't you remember? Where'd it all go so fast?"

"Maybe everyone ran out at the same time or else everyone is eating a lot of peanut butter sandwiches this week."

"Maybe someone stole it," cried Andy.

"I doubt that, Kitten. You watch. This next case will last us a month."

Andy still thought there was something wrong. As she stamped the jars, she decided to watch the peanut butter shelf whenever she could. Then, if she was right, she'd be the one to catch the thief.

After school on Monday she started. None had been sold during the day and none were sold right up to closing time. All jars in place.

Tuesday was a slow day all around — from getting up, to going to school late, to listening to the visiting librarian tell how to use the card catalog. If Andy wanted a book, she knew right where her favorite one was. She read it every visit to the library.

When she finally got to the store, there were only two customers and only one jar of crunchy peanut butter gone. She figured that made sense. She wiped out the milk case because it was right across from her shelf. Then she swept the floor in that aisle. Nothing happened.

By Wednesday Andy was getting tired of looking at peanut butter. She checked the shelf on the way in and saw that no more jars were gone. Then she filled out every item along the aisle. There were no customers in the store. Trooper Martin was up front having his daily chat with her mother. Ted had come in with her from school and was playing around out in the back.

Then the bell rang, giving the signal inside that a car was out at the gas pump. Andy ran up the aisle and out the door as fast as she could. Her father sometimes let her work the pump if he was in a good mood. He was. He left Andy to hold the gas nozzle. Mrs. Mac went on into the store for groceries. Andy knew rich, old Mrs. Mac wasn't likely to steal any peanut butter, not with this big fancy car.

Andy went back into the store, wiping her hands on her pants. She thought it was time for a piece of baloney. She saw Mrs. Mac at the checkout counter and reported the cost of the gas to her mother. Halfway toward the rear of the store she stopped, dead Her eyes turned back to the left. There—right at eye level—was a big hole where at least five jars of crunchy peanut butter had been no more than five minutes ago.

It must be old Mrs. Mac, but the jars weren't on the checkout counter, thought Andy. Nobody else has been in the store. *Why* would she steal something as dumb as peanut butter? She could buy all she wanted, and she didn't even look like someone who'd like it.

Andy raced out the back door to her bicycle parked up against the side wall. If she hurried, she could beat Mrs. Mac to her house. Andy pedaled as fast as she could down the village green. Mrs. Mac had one of the big, white houses right at the four corners.

She left her bike behind the big hedge at the end of the drive. Then, crouching, she sneaked behind the hedge toward the garage. She knew Mrs. Mac had Mildred Burly working for her in the kitchen. If Andy could get around to the back side of the garage before the car came, she could get to the kitchen window by following the hedge.

Andy crept through a newly planted bed of spring bulbs. At least she guessed it had just been planted. She could smell from her feet that the manure had been spread on the top. She reached the window, which was a good two feet above her head. The garbage can was underneath it a bit to the right. She carefully rolled it on its side edge until it was right under the window. Just in time she dove down behind the can. Mrs. Mac drove into the garage. In seconds she came tottering up the path to the back door and let herself in.

Andy carefully climbed, knee first, on top of the can. She could just see over the window ledge. Mrs. Mac dropped her grocery bag on the kitchen table and called out to Mildred that she was home. Andy was glad it wasn't quite time for the winter windows yet, because she could see and hear what was going on. Mrs. Mac started opening the bag. Andy didn't expect to see the peanut butter come out, but she'd have to take it out of her coat pockets or her tote bag soon.

Andy put one foot on top of the garbage can to boost herself up a little. Just as she put her weight on it, her foot slipped. Andy grabbed for the window sill. But the can fell over with a loud clatter and Andy crashed down on top of it. She and the coffee grounds, the orange peels — the whole mess — became one pile.

Mrs. Mac let out a hoot and the next second she and Mildred Burly were standing over Andy.

"Andrea Lowe, what in the world do you think you're doing? Get out of my garbage this minute!" Mrs. Mac exploded.

"Yes'm," mumbled Andy. Here she was with the store thief catching her instead of the other way around. She had to think. If she could get into the kitchen, she might still find the missing jars.

"I'm sorry, Mrs. Mac, but I thought I saw a coon going for your can and I dove at it. Maybe I should come inside and wash up some?"

"Andy, that's a fib and you know it. No coon's coming out in broad daylight. You come inside, but you are going to tell me what you're up to."

Mildred Burly pushed Andy along by the back of her neck. As Andy went through the doorway, she stripped off her jacket.

"All right, give me those stinking shoes and that jacket." Mildred held them far in front of her as she carried them to the laundry room sink in back of the kitchen.

Mrs. Mac settled herself down opposite Andy at the kitchen table and gave her a stern look. "Now, Andrea, let's have it. What were you after, following me from the store and spying at the window?"

Maybe I can trick her by surprise, thought Andy. "Do you like crunchy or smooth-style peanut butter better, Mrs. Mac?"

"The smooth. The crunchy kind always gets caught in my teeth. But what has that to do with the mess you made of my garbage? And don't tell me you're

16

taking a survey."

Her answer came so fast that it had to be true. Andy suddenly felt very silly. This rich, old lady couldn't be a thief. And she, Andy, wasn't going to be a big heroine. In fact, it was all so silly, she started to giggle. Mrs. Mac smiled a little.

By the time Mildred came in from the back, the two of them were sitting there laughing out loud. Mildred wasn't the least bit amused and handed Andy her sneakers and jacket with a huff. Andy and Mrs. Mac decided to have a glass of milk and some cookies while Andy tried to explain.

As they nibbled on the chocolate chips, Andy found herself telling the whole story about the store thief and about how her father wouldn't believe that someone would be silly enough to steal such a dumb thing.

"Who else was in the store, Andy? It's really quite simple. You saw the jars and then you didn't. It wasn't me, but someone had to be there to take them."

"But no one else was there. Just you." Andy stopped; her mouth hung open.

"What is it, Andy?"

"You don't think it could have been him do you?"

"Who is him?" asked Mrs. Mac.

I can't tell her, thought Andy. She'd only laugh if I said Trooper Martin. But he was the only other person there.

"Oh, no one you'd know, Mrs. Mac. I must not have been watching as well as I thought I was."

"Maybe if you keep on trying, you'll solve the mystery," said Mrs. Mac with a nod.

"Yes, I'll keep on trying, hard," said Andy with determination. "I've got to get back now or Mom'll deduct from my pay today."

Andy quickly put on her damp sneakers and jacket. With a wave and a thanks for the cookies, she ran out to recover her bicycle. Mrs. Mac made her promise to let her know of any developments or clues.

As Andy pedaled back to the store, she was so excited she nearly hit old Zeke, the dog who belonged to the Congregational minister.

Trooper Martin, she thought. Who ever would believe it? It had to be him. There was no one, absolutely no one else in the store.

Andy had seen TV shows where there were crooked policemen. They always got caught in the end, but Andy wondered how she was going to catch Trooper Martin all alone.

I can't tell anyone, thought Andy. They'd think I was crazy. But it has to be him, and I've just got to prove it.

She parked her bike and went in the back door and straight down the aisle to the front counter.

18

"Mom, what was Trooper Martin in here for this afternoon?"

"To get his paper, of course, why else?" Mrs. Lowe was sorting out the slips in the cash drawer. There were no charge accounts allowed at the market. But everyone in town had a slip in the drawer when they forgot their money or ran out. Andy thought that was a screwy way of having no charge accounts, but Mom said you had to rely on people's good will in this business.

"He didn't buy anything?" asked Andy rather hopefully. "Like maybe some peanut butter?"

"Mrs. Martin does all their shopping on Fridays. You know that." Mrs. Lowe put down her slips and frowned at Andy. "What do you have churning in that mind of yours?"

"Well, you know I told Dad the other day that some-one was stealing peanut butter, and he . . ." Before Andy could finish, her mother's laugh seemed to hit the back meat counter and bounce back. I knew I shouldn't have said anything until I caught him, thought Andy.

"And you think Trooper Martin is stealing your peanut butter?" Mrs. Lowe was laughing so hard her face was red and Andy thought it was suddenly ugly. Andy gritted her teeth hard.

"I'm sorry, Kitten. It's just that it's so silly." She reached across the counter and put her hand on Andy's arm. "First of all, I don't believe anyone is stealing peanut butter and secondly, I'm sure Trooper Martin would never steal anything."

"Sure," muttered Andy. "I guess you're right." She drew her arm back and sighed, "Guess I better finish sweeping out in the back."

She started for the back room. Maybe Ted's still here, she thought. He'd believe me. But Ted had gone home and Andy was left with her broom and her own plans to make.

As Andy swept, she thought. Trooper Martin must still have all their peanut butter jars in his car. She looked up at the clock over the meat counter. Five thirty-five. Trooper Martin was probably in his little office. That meant his car would be parked out in front of the town hall. It was just down past the monument, a little way from Mrs. Mac's house.

It was now or never. Andy knew he had to have the

20

stolen goods in his car, and she might never get another chance to catch him. She threw the broom into the corner in the back room. She stumbled on a crate and then nearly closed her fingers in the door. She was shaking and she was scared for the first time. Trooper Martin had a gun, and if she found the stuff he had stolen, he might get desperate.

She wheeled her bicycle out of the store parking lot and flung herself on it with a feeling more of doom than excitement.

It seemed to take so long to get to town hall that Andy was sure Trooper Martin would have left to go home for supper. She left her bike against Mrs. Mac's fence and walked down the road cautiously. His car was there, parked in the back by the side of the hall.

She looked around hopefully, but there was no one to see her or stop her from looking in the car. Aside from the trooper's small office upstairs, the town hall was used only for committee meetings and at voting time. It was even too small to use for the town meetings they had once or twice a year.

Andy strolled down the driveway and approached the police car. She took the side away from the hall and crouched down as she got to the car. If anyone came, she'd have the car to hide behind and the bush fence at her back.

She inched up to the window level and peered

through the back window. There were some tools on the floor and on the back seat what appeared to be a small cage. Next to it was a paper bag. A grocery bag!

She moved up to the front window and saw the newspaper on the seat next to her and a very complicated looking dash board.

She had to see inside the paper bag on the back seat. Andy looked around the car and then peeked up over the front hood. She couldn't back out now. She pressed the button and grasped the car door handle and pulled. Nothing happened. She'd have to stand up to give it enough pull. If it's not locked, she suddenly thought.

I'll do it with one quick pull, she decided. Then if it doesn't open, I'll know it's locked and get out of here fast. Up. Pull. Andy was flung backward into the bushes as the car door gave way.

"After anything special, Andy?"

Looking up at Trooper Martin from a sitting position was even worse than looking up at him standing. He was nine feet tall and his wide-brimmed hat just needed a point on top to be a witch's hat.

Andy was so frightened she couldn't speak. Her mouth wouldn't open and she couldn't breath.

"Come on, Andy, get up off that damp ground and tell me what you thought you were doing or going to do." He put his hands under her arms and propped her up against the fence.

Andy could feel her knees crumbling under her, and she grabbed the car door in front of her.

"Andy, speak." Trooper Martin looked down on her. "Better yet, breathe first, then speak."

"I'm sorry. I'm sorry," stammered Andy. "But I'm not sorry. You're the thief, not me!" she blurted. Then she tried to break past him, thinking she might be able to make it to Mrs. Mac's before he started shooting.

"Whoa, lady." He stuck out his long arms and Andy was caught. She was too scared even to struggle. "Come on, let's you and me go upstairs and have a talk. Now, no running away or you'll be obstructing justice."

"Justice," said Andy as he pushed her ahead of him up the stairs. "How come it's justice and O.K. for you to steal from our store?"

"Andy, not so fast. First of all, I didn't steal from your store. But secondly, you just can't go around accusing people. Me or anyone else. You've got to have evidence."

"That's what I was after," said Andy. "Then I'll have some evidence." She had felt a moment of courage again, but then by the end of the sentence they were standing in his office. Her accusation

24

ended in a shaky voice and wasn't very threatening.

"O.K., Andy, let's get this straightened out. What are you investigating? What's missing? Why you? Your mother didn't say a word to me earlier."

"But she didn't know you were taking the peanut butter. Only I saw you. Well, not exactly saw you, but it had to be you."

Andy couldn't escape, so she plunged ahead. Maybe Trooper Martin could explain or return the goods. Andy told her story, watching the trooper's face closely for signs of guilt.

When she got to the part about looking in his car, she said, "You have a big grocery bag on the back seat, and I figured that's where my peanut butter is now." She finished weakly. It was beginning to sound a little stupid again.

"Well, you had no business opening my car, Andy. That's against the law. If you suspect someone of stealing, you can't take the law in your own hands and break into the person's property. You certainly know better. As for the bag, it's filled with birdfood and suet for the back feeder here. I brought it from home and forgot to put it out this morning." He reached for the pipe on his desk and tapped it clean. "Back to your thief. You now have no suspects. If no one was there to take it, the peanut butter couldn't have disappeared. Maybe if you ask your father, you'll find he moved it or some such thing. I'm sure he'll have a good explanation, and if not, he can call me. I'll talk to him about it." Trooper Martin stood up and moved to the door. "But you are out of the police business as of now. If I hear one word about you sneaking around, I'll report the whole episode to your mother and father."

I'm dismissed, thought Andy. She stammered a stiff good-bye and fled down the stairs. Wow, what a let down, she grumbled to herself. She'd made a fool of herself and was caught in the bargain, and Trooper Martin now thought she was some dumb kid. Feeling very down and suddenly very tired, she walked slowly to get her bicycle.

I know the peanut butter was taken this afternoon, thought Andy. I did see it and then not see it. I have to find a suspect.

As she dragged her feet along, she tried to remember the store early this afternoon. Ted. Maybe Ted saw someone she'd missed. She started off on her way home, and as her tired legs pumped, she kept thinking: Ted, Ted, Ted.

Suddenly Andy skidded to a stop and bounced off her seat. "Why, that goon!" she screamed. "Wait'll I get my hands on him. It's got to be Ted. He's pulling a trick on me." Andy saw the whole thing clearly in her mind. Ted had been the only one in the store except Mom and Dad. "I'll beat it out of him for making me look like a jerk." She stomped on her bicycle pedal.

Then a better thought came to her. Evidence. Trooper Martin said you had to have evidence. She decided she'd follow Ted after school the next day. She'd be waiting for him at home and trail him after he changed his school clothes. She'd get even.

Thursday was usually a good day for Andy. She had gym in the afternoon, and it was "little Friday." That was Andy's own way of counting only one more day to the weekend. But today the hours seemed to drag.

It was easy for Andy to get out of her gym class early. It was her favorite subject, and when she told Mrs. Barnum she felt sick and wanted to go home, it didn't for a minute occur to the gym teacher to doubt her. Andy felt awful about the lie.

Andy showered and got out of the school building quickly since no one else was in the hall. She rode by the store and stuck her head just inside.

"Mom, if it's O.K., I'm going to skip work today."

"What's the matter, don't you feel well?"

"Oh, sure. I just have a project I have to get done." Andy didn't think that was a lie, since seeing what Ted was up to was going to be a project.

When Andy got home, she carefully put her bicycle

out behind the barn so she could get to it quickly and unseen. Next she had to find a hiding place where Ted wouldn't see her, but where she could watch him.

She stood looking around the kitchen. He had to come and leave through here. But there was just no hiding place that would do. Finally she thought of a way.

She ran to the linen closet and dug through until she found the big linen table cloth they used for Thanksgiving and Christmas. She struggled to unfold it and get it over the kitchen table. It looked kind of messy since the cloth was long and the table was round. But it did cover all the way down to the floor, with a lot hanging down in the back. Andy flew under the table when she saw Ted riding into the driveway. She fixed the drape so she could just peek out or pull back and be safely hidden.

Ted came in fast, but then he always did everything too fast her father said.

He threw his books on the table over Andy's head. Then there was a silence, and she could see his hand lift up the front corner of the big table cloth. She held her breath and shut her eyes.

He didn't look under. He dropped the cloth corner and moved to the other side of the kitchen.

Andy peered out under the edge and watched. Ted

took off his sweater and threw it on a chair. He grabbed the kitchen stool and went right up to the broom closet shelf and took down five boxes of sugar. Then he ran out of the room, and Andy could hear him pounding up the stairs. She decided to stay where she was and wait because he had started something here.

Ted came back into the kitchen in one minute carrying five jars of peanut butter. That was all Andy needed. She whipped up the cloth and then sprawled forward with a crash as she got all tangled up trying to get out. Her leg had lost all its feeling and she was lying face down on the kitchen floor. She couldn't blame Ted for dropping the jars or for letting out a terrifying yell. Then his face clouded up and he began to cry!

Andy hadn't seen Ted cry in years. He was always so calm and so tough.

She scrambled up and limped over to him, not even remembering she was mad at him. She threw her arm around his shoulder. "Ted, it's O.K. It'll all work out. Stop the tears. Come on."

"It's not O.K. Now you'll tell everybody about me. You're supposed to be at the store and not here." His tears stopped and he glared at Andy as if she were the one doing wrong.

"The reason I'm not at the store, you sneak, is be-

cause you're pulling tricks on me and making me look foolish to everybody," snapped Andy.

Ted looked puzzled and asked, "Tricks? What tricks? What are you talking about?"

"Well," said Andy triumphantly, "for starters, I've caught you with the peanut butter that I thought someone was stealing."

"I wasn't tricking you. I needed it."

"What are you doing with all this stuff anyway?" Andy's hand swept over the piles of sugar and peanut butter.

Ted's face clouded again. "That's what I don't want you to tell anybody. I've been making the fudge Mrs. Tunney sells at the school cafeteria."

"You? All by yourself?" Andy was flabbergasted.

"Remember, I mowed Mrs. Tunney's lawn last summer and we got talking one day. She said no one ever bothered to make homemade fudge anymore. So she and I made some. Then we got to talking about how it was harder to earn any extra money during the winter months. I said maybe if I made fudge, she could sell it in the cafeteria," Ted explained quietly. Then he mumbled even lower. "But I didn't want anyone to know I was making the fudge. Everybody would laugh at me."

"I'm not laughing at you. Why, you're in business. I think that's very clever." Andy's mental cash register was ticking away. "Where do you make it?" she asked.

"I take the stuff over to Mrs. Tunney's twice a week and do it. Then she cuts it and wraps it after it's cool and takes it into school. She swore to keep my secret. She slips me the money at the end of the week. This is only my second week making it, though."

"Wow, is that ever smart and you get fifteen cents for every one of those little packages at school. You'll be rich, Ted."

"No, I won't. Not now. Everyone will know and I won't make it anymore." He looked sadly at Andy.

"You're not going to stop, dumb-dumb. You're going to expand!"

Ted's eyes widened as Andy whirled around the kitchen.

"What do you mean?" he asked.

"Don't you see? I keep quiet about it, but I'm your new 'silent partner'. I'll keep your secret and bring the groceries to you. But even better, I'm going to be your saleswoman."

"What's that mean?" asked Ted suspiciously.

"Wherever I can sell your fudge other than the cafeteria, I get half of the profits," answered Andy, slapping her hands on her jeans.

"But where are you going to sell it?"

"How about Scout meetings, the high school games, and maybe even the store when we decide to let Mom and Pop in on it? That's just for starters!" Andy was jumping with excitement.

"Yeah, but I'm going to have to make all that fudge," answered Ted crossly.

"Dumb-dumb, when it gets to be a big deal, you'll be the owner. Then you can hire other kids to do the work. Ted, you'll be so rich, nobody can laugh at you." Andy could see it now—world-wide: 'Andy & Ted's Candies'.

"Hey, wait a sec. I started out to make some quiet pocket money. But you're taking over and running everything."

"Don't you want to be rich and famous?" shouted Andy.

"Not really," replied Ted. "I just want a little extra money."

"You'll have lots extra, and when it's really going, you won't even have to work. You'll just be boss."

Andy wouldn't give up, and she finally talked Ted into giving the partnership a try.

The next week was really busy, between lugging home the groceries to Ted on her bicycle and taking orders for A & T Fudge. She saw Mrs. Mac at the store twice, but she ducked into the back room. Andy didn't want to tell her the whole story until she and Ted were really on their way, and the fudge maker could be revealed.

It was the following Friday after school when Andy breezed into the store and smacked right into Trooper Martin. Her mother was talking to him and looked very excited.

"Andy, there you are. Well, you were right. We do have a thief."

"But, Mom, there's no thief. It was all a mistake. I just thought there was." Andy looked nervously at Trooper Martin. She wondered if he'd told her mom and dad about her silly sleuthing.

35

"No, someone *has* been stealing from us. We're going through all the shelves tonight to see what's missing." Mother sounded worried.

"We've just been using a lot at home. . . ." Andy rushed on happily.

"Don't be silly, dear. We always write down what we take. We don't run off with things without paying," Mom answered shortly.

Andy hesitated. "We do. I mean, we don't? But it's our store."

"When we take groceries, it's part of your father's salary and I keep very good records." Mother sounded impatient.

Andy went rigid. That meant *they'd* been stealing. She and Ted. Andy's mother started down the aisle with the trooper and Andy turned and stumbled for the door.

She had to get to Ted. He was probably still at school waiting for Mrs. Tunney to settle his weekly bill. She always paid him after everyone had left on Friday. But Andy couldn't let Mrs. Tunney find out. She would tell the school principal and then they'd be expelled. It was bad enough that they were going to jail.

Andy started running around to the back for her bicycle. Mrs. Mac's big silver-gray car pulled in behind the gas pump. Andy had to dodge her.

36

But Mrs. Mac was not to be dodged. She rolled down her window and yelled after Andy. When Andy kept on going, Mrs. Mac started blowing her horn.

"I'm not allowed to start the gas pump, Mrs. Mac," she called between gulps for air.

"Andy, I don't want you to pump the gas. I want to know why you've been hiding every time I come into the store. I thought we were friends."

Andy started to pedal again. She couldn't look Mrs. Mac in the eye. "Talk to you later," she called as she escaped out the driveway.

Andy went as fast as she could and had to skid to a halt for the stop sign at the monument. She felt guilty as she went by Mrs. Mac's house. She had not been very polite just now and Mrs. Mac was only trying to be nice. She was the only one who had paid any attention to her in the beginning of this mess.

As Andy passed town hall, she wondered again if Trooper Martin had told on her for trying to get into his car. For someone with a dull life, I've managed to get into a lot of trouble, thought Andy.

The school yard was empty except for Mrs. Tunney's car, the janitor's green pick-up truck and Ted's bicycle in the rack. Andy slid off hers and ran it between the slats in the stand.

She went to the back door which led directly into the cafeteria kitchen. It made Andy think of a hos-

pital as she passed through the cold, empty stainless steel cavern. She heard Mrs. Tunney's hearty voice coming from her little office on the side.

Andy looked around the corner of the doorway and could have kicked Ted. He was sitting across the desk from Mrs. Tunney, grinning happily. She could hardly wait to tell him he was going to jail.

"Psst!" She waved her hand and hissed to get his attention. "Psst."

Mrs. Tunney turned around at the same time that Ted saw her. His grin spread as he held up the envelope of money he had.

"Come on in. I'm just telling Mrs. Tunney about your great ideas."

"Hi, Andy. Come in. I can't wait to hear more." Mrs. Tunney swiveled her chair to face the doorway.

"Your mom and dad must be very proud to see you two working together in your own little business." She looked all ready for a nice long chat.

"Oh," Ted started to say, "they don't . . ."

"They don't pay much attention," said Andy, quickly cutting Ted out with a loud voice. "But that's why I've come for Ted. We have to hurry. Something very important has come up. Something that can't wait." She had stepped into the room while she talked and had Ted firmly by the elbow and was pulling him out of his chair.

"We'll see you next week, Mrs. Tunney." I hope, she thought desperately. "Come on, Ted. We have to go." She dragged the stumbling Ted out as he said a quick good-bye to Mrs. Tunney. He waved his envelope and yelled back, "Thanks, again."

"Andy, you're crazy!" He pulled his arm free, but kept up with her as she ran out the back door.

"Get your bike and let's get out of here," she snapped.

He followed her out of the school yard and down the road. She picked a spot in the road before the bend would put them in view of town hall. Then she pulled over to the side and waited for Ted to stop next to her.

"We are in terrible trouble!" She gasped for breath. "Both of us, but me more because I'm older."

"What's that got to do with it? And what do you mean we're in trouble? For what?" he asked.

"We've been stealing." Her voice shook as she said it aloud for the first time.

"I didn't steal anything. What'd you steal? he asked calmly.

"Peanut butter, chocolate, milk, sugar. What do you think I'm talking about?" Andy exploded.

"But we're not stealing," said Ted in a very pious tone. "It's our store. We always just take stuff from it."

"That's just it, dumb-dumb. We aren't supposed to do that." She quickly told Ted how Mom and Dad kept track of all they took home and now were checking stock to see what was missing. She described Trooper Martin at the store looking for clues to the thief.

"It's all my fault. If I'd talked to Mom and Pop about your fudge from the beginning, we wouldn't be thieves. I've been sneaking the stuff past them." Andy sat in the leaves on the road side.

"No, it's my fault. I'm the one who started it all. I'll give myself up." Ted was looking bravely in the direction of the town hall. "Maybe I should just go away somewhere. I could get a job and pay back what we took."

"Dumb-dumb, what kind of a job can you get? And running away is just another wrong thing, and anyway, it wouldn't work." Andy sifted the leaves through her fingers as she sat and thought.

"I've been galloping around town trying so hard for some excitement and all I've done is mess up your business and make us into criminals." Andy stood up and groaned. "It's time I really straightened this out and got back to my nice dull life. I don't want to feel guilty all the time. I'm going to confess."

"Not without me, you're not. We're partners and you're not very 'silent'. I guess my fudge business is

finished for good," Ted said mournfully.

"Finished?" snorted Andy. "Listen, if I can confess and take the blame for stealing, the least you can do is own up to your fudge-making."

The ride back to the store seemed short and they met only one car on the road. Trooper Martin was coming from the store on his way to his office. Andy waved a weak salute. He'd find out about the crime soon enough, she thought. Imagine, she had accused him of stealing and here she was a thief herself.

It was just five-thirty when they rode into the parking lot. Andy had a queer feeling as they entered the store through the front door. She felt very protective of Ted and wanted her parents to understand it wasn't his fault. She should have stopped him when she found out about it or at least have confided in them. She also had a sense of relief. She hadn't really liked having such a big secret from everyone. Small ones, yes. They were necessary in order to have your own thoughts.

Mrs. Lowe had the big order book out and was bent over the counter taking the sheets out one by one.

"Mom, I can help." Andy stared at the top of her mother's head.

"Hi, Kitten. Thanks for the offer, but this will be an all night job for us. You could be a help if you'd warm up some soup and make sandwiches for you and Ted. And no TV after nine o'clock." She said the last with a tired smile at Andy. "You better go on home before too long."

"I mean, I really *can* help," said Andy. "I can tell you what's missing."

"Why, Kitten, I know you've been watching the shelves, but you'd never know every item. Ben Martin says he wants to know exactly what's missing to see if whoever is doing it has some kind of a pattern."

"I can tell you exactly, too," said Ted. He reached for Andy's hand as he continued. "I can show you my recipe."

"Your what?" asked Mrs. Lowe.

"We took it and it's my fault," said Andy. She wasn't going to let Ted take the blame.

"You took what?" asked Mrs. Lowe. For the first time she gave her full attention.

Andy started way back with the peanut butter. The minute she got to Ted it seemed to get jumbled.

44

Her mother started asking all kinds of questions and finally stopped her only when the bell rang for a gas customer outside.

"Hold it, Andy. This sounds as if we'd better get Daddy. You two go in the back and wait. We'll talk it all out just as soon as we lock up."

Andy started automatically for a piece of baloney at the meat counter. That's what she always did when she was hungry or bored or felt sorry for herself. Then she stopped. No taking food, she thought. She and Ted both sat down quietly next to the butcher's block and waited.

Finally Andy could hear the low voices of her parents from up in the front. She guessed her mother was filling her father in on what they'd done. She really wished she could tell him herself, but she decided she'd better stay put. She heard the door being locked, and then she saw the front outside lights go off. Then her parents came down the aisle toward them.

"How about a piece of baloney, Kitten?" her father's voice was quiet.

"But that's just it," cried Andy. "Why is it O.K. to take a piece of baloney, but it's not O.K. to take everything else?"

"It's not O.K., Andy. One is no different than the other." He looked sad and Andy was surprised because she figured he should be mad.

"It's not?" Andy looked puzzled.

"Then we *didn't* steal," said Ted firmly.

"Yes, Ted, you and Andy stole from our store. It was not right for you to just take groceries without telling us. You see, any food we take is really part of my income and should be in all my account books."

"But you said Andy should have some baloney." Now Ted sounded confused.

"I know. I did it for a reason," said his father. "Mom told me your story and you *were* dishonest in taking the food. You, particularly, Andy, were selfish in not taking the time to think it through, but you only thought of your own interests."

Andy wanted to cry. In fact, she was about to burst. Then she looked her father in the eye and knew he was forgiving her.

"It was for me she did it." Ted's voice was small.

"Let me finish, Ted. I asked Andy if she wanted the baloney to show you that your mother and I feel that some of the blame is ours. We do keep a record of our food, but a slice of baloney or sometimes an orange drink gets forgotten. This is our mistake, and we take the blame for not being careful of our own actions." When he had finished, his arms were around both of them.

"You mean we don't have to go to jail, or report to Trooper Martin?" asked Andy, letting a big gust of wind out of her throat.

"No, Kitten," said her mother. "I think we can work all of this out tonight at home. I want to hear more about this fudge business, and I want a piece!" Mrs. Lowe had put on her coat and was handing her husband his jacket.

"I haven't got any, but I can take . . ." Ted stopped and looked stricken.

"I'll get the stuff," Andy yelled as she bounded up the aisle. "*And* put it on a slip in the 'no charge account' drawer!"